THE DEEP END DEMON

THE DEEP END DEMON

Jason M. Burns

DARBY CREEK
MINNEAPOLIS

Darby Creek
An imprint of Lerner Publishing Group, Inc.
241 First Avenue North
Minneapolis, MN 55401 USA

For reading levels and more information, look up this title at www.lernerbooks.com.

Image credits: Vladimir Mulder/Shutterstock (cover); Rosen Graphic/Shutterstock (texture); idwan kurnia/Shutterstock (font); PERFECT_VECTORS/Shutterstock (font).

Main body text set in Janson Text LT Std.
Typeface provided by Adobe Systems.

Library of Congress Cataloging-in-Publication Data

Names: Burns, Jason M., 1978–author
Title: The deep end demon / Jason M. Burns.
Description: Minneapolis : Darby Creek, 2026. | Series: Demon hunter | Audience term: Teenagers | Audience: Ages 11–18 | Audience: Grades 7–9 | Summary: When two kids go missing from the water park, Damon and his demon-hunting friends set out to rescue them from a pirate-loving kappa.
Identifiers: LCCN 2025012872 (print) | LCCN 2025012873 (ebook) | ISBN 9798765670682 library binding | ISBN 9798348028213 paperback | ISBN 9798765691977 epub
Subjects: CYAC: Demons—Fiction | Kappa (Japanese water goblin)—Fiction | Ability—Fiction | Friendship—Fiction | Salem (Mass.)—Fiction | LCGFT: Paranormal fiction | Novels
Classification: LCC PZ7.1.B88535 De 2026 (print) | LCC PZ7.1.B88535 (ebook) | DDC [Fic]—dc23/eng/20250320

LC record available at https://lccn.loc.gov/2025012872
LC ebook record available at https://lccn.loc.gov/2025012873

Manufactured in the United States of America
1 – TR – 12/15/25

To Hunter and Eloise—hunt down what makes you happy in life and don't be afraid to face your demons.

1

The waves crash into me. They slap against my face, tearing the breath from my lungs. I feel my body growing more exhausted with each passing wave. My muscles are giving out. I'm sinking. The only part of me left above the surface of the water is my face, and now that too is . . .

"Damon, what are you doing?" Madelyn asks, standing outside of the wave pool beneath a large patio umbrella.

I climb up from my knees and stand. I'm currently in the shallow end of Captain Froggerton's Wonderful Wave Pool, letting my imagination get the better of me. I lean my head to one side and let the water drain out of my ear.

"Sorry," I say, climbing the steps to exit the wave pool. The concrete surrounding the pool singes my feet and I run to the shade beneath Madelyn's umbrella. "I can't resist a good pirate fantasy. In my mind, I was just forced to walk the plank."

Madelyn looks out over the wave pool. With a maximum depth of four feet, it's the most popular attraction for younger kids at Captain Froggerton's Water World. My friends and I came to the park for the extreme waterslides, but my inner child always has a hard time keeping out of the waves. It's a classic.

"Do you have any idea how much urine is in there?" Madelyn asks.

Liam finds his way into the conversation, making sure to stop short of the umbrella's shade. He's carrying three tricolored popsicles in his hands. "I don't even have a bladder, but I know a wave pool is basically a public toilet. I already saw one kid lose his diaper in there."

It might sound a bit odd to hear that my best friend doesn't have a bladder, but in my world, it's probably one of the tamest things you could hear us talk about throughout an average day.

You see, Liam is a demon. And while some of his teachers may call him a demon in a tongue-in-cheek, "he's so difficult in the classroom" sort of way, I know the truth. He is a 100 percent born and bred spawn of The Pit in the underworld.

He's also about a foot taller than anyone in our grade and is built like a Greek Spartan. His abs have abs. With both of our shirts off, I look like a snuggly teddy bear standing next to him.

I go to take one of the popsicles from Liam. He recoils.

"Get your own," he says, licking all three of the pops simultaneously. "Besides, you've been tainted by the pee pool. I'm not letting you touch me until you rinse off in the showers."

Liam's bare feet are pressed comfortably into the blazing hot concrete. The temperatures of Salem, Massachusetts—even on the hottest of days—pale in comparison to those where Liam is from. I wouldn't be surprised if his feet were even a bit chilly against the sunbaked ground.

Even for Madelyn, this hot July day is probably considered mild. She's originally from Texas, so she's used to the heat. She's not wearing a head-to-toe wet suit because she's cold. She's wearing it because she was born with albinism.

Her skin is extremely pale and that makes being in the sun—even for a few minutes—dangerous. It's why her parents moved her up here a few years ago. Salem isn't always dreary, but it's also not as close to the equator as Texas. At least up here in Massachusetts, the sun's rays aren't as intense.

"So, what should we hit up first?" Madelyn asks as she applies a fresh layer of sunscreen to her face. Her freckles disappear beneath the thick coating of SPF.

I look out over the wave pool, longing to play out the rest of my pirate adventure. I see a young boy—no more than eight—driving his chest into the continuous onslaught of waves. He wears a play eye patch and yells "ARGH" as each wave thumps against his body.

A kid after my own heart.

I turn to Madelyn as she snaps the cap of her sunscreen closed. "I always like to begin and end my day here with a few laps on Captain Froggerton's Lazy River," I say. "Any objections?"

"Works for me," Madelyn says.

Liam bites down on one of the popsicle's wooden sticks. His teeth scrape against it, causing goose bumps to ripple over my flesh. "As long as we eventually ride the new Devil's Plunge waterslide, I don't care what we do."

As we head out for the lazy river, I turn to look back at the wave pool. My fellow pirate lover is no longer braving the waters. I glance around, looking to see where he wandered off to, but I can't seem to locate him. Maybe he had some friends talk him out of having a little pirate fun, too.

2

Captain Froggerton's Zigzagging Lazy River winds through the water park, twisting in and out of the other attractions. It seamlessly blends in with the various waterslides, splash pads, and pools, offering a calming journey while floating on an oversized blow-up tube. If you don't mind the smell of chlorine while you're relaxing, it's a great way to chill out.

Liam and Madelyn are floating ahead of me. They are holding on to each other's tubes, creating a multiperson raft between them. They call it the "fun pontoon." They giggle as they are pulled beneath a waterfall meant for cooling off guests.

I'm trapped inside my own head like some of the empty inner tubes caught up in the river's slow current. I'm just . . . floating about, both inside and out.

It's nice to finally have a day off. Even though we're on summer vacation, my friends and I have been so busy lately. These hot summer nights always seem to pull the stray demons out of the woodwork.

Just to clarify, when not doing your average, everyday teenager things, my friends and I hunt demons. I know that probably sounds a bit odd seeing that I'm BFFs with one, but Liam isn't like most demons. For starters, most demons wouldn't be floating down a lazy river with me unless they were using my bloated corpse as their inner tube.

Our demon hunting is helped by the fact that I can see auras. An aura is like a fingerprint for the soul. Seeing auras is an extremely rare gift, and I didn't even know I had it until my mom realized that I could do it. She fancied herself a spiritual seeker, which meant she studied a lot of practices meant to achieve inner peace. This included meditation, crystal healing, and vibrational frequencies. She had read about those who could see auras and taught me that seeing an aura was not as important as reading one.

Trust me, there's a big difference between the two.

I can tell so much about someone by reading their aura. I know if they're a dog lover, a cat person, or if they prefer an animal-free home. I can learn more about you and your personality than you would tell me yourself. Cheated on your latest math test? I know about it. Have a crush on your lab partner? Can't hide it from me. Weaseled into the world through a magical portal so you could cause death and destruction? Nope, you're not slipping away without me noticing.

Most people don't even know that demons exist. As far as the general public is concerned, they're just movie monsters, not an actual threat. In fact, more people probably believe in werewolves and vampires than demons. (What people don't know is that there is a type of demon that is a mix of those two on-screen monsters. We have decided to call them *werepires.* They're a nasty bunch and always travel in groups of three, just like my friends and I.)

Anyway, it was my ability to see and read auras that first brought demons to my attention. That's because a human's aura looks a lot different than a demon's.

Take my two free-floating friends, for example. Above Madelyn's head, I see color and shimmer. It looks like mica, a kind of rock that Mom and I used to collect on our hikes through the White Mountains of New Hampshire.

As for Liam, his aura is more like a twisting knot of darkness and despair. His does have an important detail that stands out from other demons, though. His has the faintest hint of color—an inner glow that I call his aura's heart. It's the piece of his aura that told me he was inherently good. That's not a normal feature in the auras of other trickster demons, which is the variety of demon that Liam is.

So, when it comes to humans and demons, it really is night and day as far as auras go. I could pick a demon out in a crowd of thousands, but thankfully, I don't have to worry about that now. Today is all about rest and relaxation.

"Are you ever going to catch up?" Liam calls out from around the winding curve of the lazy river.

I lean my head back on my blow-up tube and close my eyes. "It's called a *lazy* river for a reason, Liam."

I hear nothing but splashing, squealing children as I round the curve. I know I'm passing the wave pool, and I go back to daydreaming about walking the plank. I'm just about to be saved by my dastardly crew when I hear a woman scream.

I open my eyes and look out at the wave pool as I pass by. A dark-haired woman in a sky blue tankini sprints through the lawn chairs of parents, most of whom are lost in whatever they're doing on their phones. The woman in the tankini is in a panic. She flaps her arms up and down, like a flightless bird refusing to deny herself the pleasure of the sky.

"Has anyone seen my son?!" she shouts. "He was just here a few seconds ago. I glanced down at my book, and when I looked back up again, he was gone. He was wearing a pirate eye patch!"

Liam and Madelyn are waiting for me at the exit of the lazy river. I hop off of my tube and splash down into the waist-high water.

"Did you hear that woman screaming for her missing son?" Madelyn asks.

I push my tube into the holding area where other park guests can retrieve it. The tube bumps into a handful of others and comes to a stop. It bobs up and down on the water like a seagull at rest on the sea.

"It was hard to miss," I say, climbing out of the lazy river. Water drips down from my bathing suit, returning to the river. "I think I know her kid. Well, not *know*, but I remember seeing him in the wave pool earlier."

We all watch as the nervous mother is met by a pair of Captain Froggerton's security guards. One is a tall woman whose aura is jam-packed with streaks of silver swirls. The other is a short man with an aura of crinkly pink cotton candy above his head. They try to calm the mother down long enough to gather more information, but she is absolutely frantic, and rightfully so. She just keeps pleading with the security guards to find him.

"Maybe we should look into it?" Madelyn suggests, but it's more of a question than a statement.

Liam steps out from underneath the overhang of the lazy river's exit. He positions his body in the full, blazing spotlight that is the afternoon sun. His demon instincts look to soak up as much heat as he possibly can.

"What could we do?" he asks as the water droplets covering his human skin evaporate before my eyes. "Missing kids is more of a police matter. We'd just be getting in the way."

My stomach does a series of chaotic flips, churning up my anxiety. Something feels altogether off about this. My twisting gut is telling me that this is *exactly* our kind of case.

I spot something resting by a drainage

grate in the ground not far from the wave pool. The security guards are so focused on the frightened mother that they haven't even started looking for any sort of evidence yet.

I think I just found some.

I walk toward the dropped item and pick up my pace to keep the bottoms of my feet from burning on the cement.

"Hey!" Liam shouts after me. "Where are you off to in such a hurry?"

I reach the drainage grate and bend down to investigate the discarded evidence. It's an elastic band, no thicker than the tooth of a comb. At each end of the band is a tiny knot. It's the kind of flexible strap that would be used to keep a plastic eye patch secured to someone's head. The kind of eye patch worn by an imaginative kid just out to have some fun in a wave pool.

"This belongs to the missing kid," I tell my friends as they join me. "I'm sure of it."

"Then what are you doing touching it?" Madelyn asks, her voice rising in concern. "You're putting your fingerprints all over it. If anyone knows better, it should be you."

She's right. Dad is a Salem police officer. With him being a cop, I know how these types of investigations work. You're not supposed to interfere with a crime scene in any way because that can compromise it and lead investigators in the wrong direction.

I feel the weight of my phone pressing against my thigh. I have it tucked away inside of a plastic bag to keep it from getting wet. If it were up to me, I would have just put it in one of the lockers that you can rent, but my dad expects me to have my phone on me at *all* times. He even supplied the sandwich bag this morning. He doesn't like to take any chances, especially after my mom disappeared a few years ago and never returned home.

Mom was a backup singer who went on a world tour. It was a great opportunity for her, and I was the one who convinced her she should go. But when the tour stopped in Brazil, she disappeared from her hotel room and was never found. It was only a few months ago that the Brazilian authorities officially declared her dead. My dad never recovered, and he has upped his safety game quite a bit since then. I get it, which is why I don't argue with him about it.

Madelyn is right. I do know how investigations work. But I also know what it is like to have a loved one go missing. I'm certain that this isn't the type of case that is going to fall under the jurisdiction of the police. We're the only investigators capable of returning that kid safely to his mother. And we have to help fast.

I ignore Madelyn's concern and bend down to sniff the air coming from the drainage grate. I smell decomposing fish—like sushi left out in the sun for a week—and a lingering aroma of rotten eggs and pond muck.

"I don't think the security guards or the cops will be able to handle this one," I say ominously.

"Why do you say that?" Madelyn asks.

I stick my finger through one of the holes of the drainage grate. When I bring it back, it's covered in a thick, splotchy sludge that resembles watered-down mashed potatoes. We all recognize it immediately.

"Ectoplasm," I say.

"Well, don't look at me," Liam quickly chimes in. "It's not mine."

4

Contrary to what pop culture would have you believe, ectoplasm isn't exclusive to ghosts. Ectoplasm exists wherever a spiritual being interacts with the physical world. That includes demons. The local police are not equipped to handle this kind of case. We are.

I flick the ectoplasm onto the sizzling concrete and wipe the residue onto my wet bathing suit. Before we can get a handle on exactly what is going on at Captain Froggerton's Water World, another hysterical scream pierces what should be the joyful sounds of summer.

"My daughter!" a man's voice shouts. "Please, someone help me find my daughter!"

The man pushes through us on his way to the security guards. Still trying to take the tankini woman's statement regarding her missing son, the security guards are overwhelmed. The terrified father foams at the mouth, his spittle getting trapped in his beard. He grabs the tall security guard by her hand and tries to pull her away.

"This way," the man says. The security guard digs her heels into the ground.

The shorter security guard takes a deep breath and looks over at his partner. "We should call this in."

The taller security guard breaks the man's grip on her hand and holds up her index finger, signaling for the man to give her a moment. The streaks of silver in her aura rattle like delicate vases on a shelf in an earthquake. She's nervous—unsure of herself.

She unclips the walkie-talkie from her belt and brings it up to her mouth. "Lily Pad to the Frog Pond," she says, speaking the words like someone trained to say them in a particular way. "We have a situation down here that requires police involvement. We're going to need Frog Pond to call the proper authorities over to the park immediately. Over."

"Finally, you're doing something, but it's still not enough!" the father says, his meaty midsection bumping into the shorter security guard as his panic turns to frustration. "My daughter was playing with the pirate water cannons on the south side of the park. After that, I didn't see her again. Come with me to look for her while the police are on their way!"

The shorter security guard nods.

That's weird. Two missing kids and both were playing with something pirate related. Though, I guess at a water park, it's par for the course. Even I fell into pirate daydreams based on my surroundings.

As the two panicked parents continue to fear the worst, I notice something strange behind the mass of curious onlookers who have gathered. A dark cloud floats just over everyone's head in the distance. It travels along from east to west, keeping in line with the horizon of people, all of whom are now clutching tightly to their own children. This cloud looks like one of those unsettling thunderstorm types that can pop up at a moment's notice in the summer, but I know that's not what it really is. I know because I'm the only one who can see it.

It's an aura.

My eyes remain fixed on the aura as its owner comes into view. Lean and wiry like a stretchy action figure, the middle-aged man is wearing gray coveralls. It's the kind of uniform you'd see on a mechanic. The Captain Froggerton character is embroidered on the back of the coveralls, and a peeling patch on the front of the uniform suggests that his name is Gary.

Gary is pushing a large rubber trash barrel on wheels through the park as he snacks on a cucumber. Completely oblivious to the frenzy overtaking the guests, he chomps down on the vegetable—peel and all—as he shuffles past.

He seems to be repeating something quietly to himself between chews.

My friends are suddenly aware of how hyperfocused I am on Gary.

"What do you see, Damon?" Madelyn asks.

I watch Gary as he approaches a small

building meant to blend into the park's festive surroundings. There is a mural of rainbow-colored waves painted on the concrete exterior of the building, but otherwise it's meant to go unnoticed. Gary is wheeling his barrel toward a door marked *Employees Only*.

"That maintenance man," I say, gesturing with my head in Gary's direction. "He may be maintenance, but he is no man."

We watch as Gary enters the building, pulling the barrel behind him through the doorway.

"That bin of his would make for a convenient way of moving kids around the park," Liam points out.

I nod. "That's what I was thinking, too."

"Then what are we waiting for?" Madelyn asks, moving toward the building. Liam and I hesitate, anchoring ourselves in place. She looks back at us with a raised eyebrow. "What is it?"

I shift awkwardly, my arms reaching up to cover my bare upper body. "I'm not really comfortable investigating a case like . . .

well, this."

"Same," Liam says.

Madelyn sighs. "Fine. Grab your shirts from the lockers. We're officially on the clock."

5

Back in the comfort of my V-neck T-shirt, I knock on the door intended for employees only. There is no response.

I turn to look over my shoulder at my friends. They are tucked behind me, trying to look as inconspicuous as possible. Liam, wearing a flowy orange and green Hawaiian shirt, nods to me. His nod says, "It's go time," without actually saying the words.

I grab hold of the door handle. Having been in the sun for the better part of the day, the metal knob is hot to the touch. I turn it, but it doesn't budge. The door is locked.

"Move aside," Liam says, stepping up to the door.

Liam isn't just a great friend; he's also a great asset when it comes to demon hunting. Because of his trickster ancestry, he's strong.

Like, incredibly strong. I once watched him rip a telephone pole right out of the ground and use it like a baseball bat as we squared off with a smoke demon. Sure, half of Salem lost power that day because of it, but thankfully, the downed lines were blamed on a spring storm. Also, we totally smoked that smoke demon, so it all worked out.

Liam runs his open hand over the door. He's searching for the right spot to deliver a solid strike that will break the door's lock. He finds what he's looking for and glances back at Madelyn and me.

"Anybody watching us?" he asks.

Madelyn looks back at the park patrons. The police have just arrived, so everyone is hypnotized by the swirling lights atop their cruisers. Thankfully, Captain Froggerton's Water World is located in the neighboring town of Marblehead, so I don't have to worry about running into my dad. Salem, and only Salem, is his jurisdiction. Still, he's probably tracking my whereabouts through my phone. I'd expect no less.

"Everyone is preoccupied," Madelyn says. "But let's do this quick. We need to get this over with before the police start looking around."

Liam grabs hold of the doorknob with his left hand. He pulls the door toward him as he thwacks it once with his right hand at the sweet spot he previously uncovered. The sudden force rips the door from its locked position, but Liam maintains control of it by holding firmly on to the knob. It's a beautifully stealthy break-in that brings us no added attention. Unless, of course, the demon is standing directly on the other side of the door, ready to pounce on us.

We slip in quickly, hiding ourselves away inside the wave-covered building. Liam props a box of unopened chlorine containers in front of the door to keep it from swinging open now that it's broken.

The room we're standing in is no bigger than a walk-in pantry closet. Our shoulders touch as we wedge ourselves into the center of a circle created by a series of industrial warehouse shelving. Stocked with cleaning supplies, the shelves line the room on three sides, stopping only at the fourth wall where there is a flight of concrete steps. The steps lead down, beneath the park. Although Gary is nowhere to be seen, I peek over the railing to see that his barrel is tipped over at the bottom of the staircase.

"What do you think is down there?" I ask, unsure of what is typically found beneath a water park.

Madelyn shakes her head. "For a place this massive to function, especially with all of the water it needs to stay running, it takes a complex web of filtration systems, pipes, and pumps. I'd imagine it's like a labyrinth down there."

Liam stands at the top of the concrete staircase, looking down into the darkness. "Sounds like a pretty good demon lair to me." He turns to look back at us. "Are we ready to flush him out?"

Madelyn and I nod.

"Okay," Liam says, descending the concrete

staircase. "I'll take point. You two stick close behind. Other than his love for cucumbers—which is a totally weird snack for a carnivorous demon, by the way—we have no idea what type of demon we're dealing with. I don't want either of you getting hurt."

The three of us make our way down into the sublevel of the park. Liam leads the way with Madelyn in the middle and me pulling up the rear. At the bottom of the stairs, I kneel down to investigate the overturned barrel. I expect to find it lined with sludge and streaked with trash water, but it's spotless inside. The barrel might as well be brand-new.

"Well, he certainly wasn't hauling trash in this thing," I say.

Suddenly, we hear a distant scream muffled by the deep and winding tunnels. The scream is unmistakably one of terror and most certainly belongs to a child.

"Let's go!" I shout, running off into the darkness of the tunnels.

It's difficult to make heads or tails of where we are. The tunnels are dark, lit only by the eerie red glow of the occasional exit sign. Pipes line the walls and the continuous flow of water inside of them is creating the kind of white noise that seems artificial, like a sound machine meant to help a baby drift off to sleep. The air reeks of chemicals.

"What is that smell?" I ask.

Madelyn sniffs at the air, confirming her senses. "It's probably a combination of chlorine and other chemicals used in the park's water filtration system."

I pull my shirt up over my nose.

Liam stops. He looks around the tunnels.

"What is it?" I ask.

"We have no idea where we're even going," Liam says. His frustration is as crystal clear as the pools and slides. "And the scream stopped, so we don't have anything to follow."

I move ahead of Liam and inspect what appears to be a footprint on the floor of the tunnel. "We can't give up on those missing kids. We're the only ones who can help them. The police will have no idea what they're dealing with."

The footprint belongs to a boot, and the brand's logo is visible in the outline of the treads. Although there is only one, it does appear to be pointed in the same direction that we are headed in.

"I'm not sure if it belongs to our demon, but this print is heading where we are," I say. "It's the best clue we've got and worth following."

Before either of my friends can respond, a high-pitched squeaking can be heard coming from the darkness of the tunnel up ahead. It begins faintly but grows louder and louder with each thump of my heartbeat. I'm suddenly aware of how much I dislike being stuck in a confined space.

"Sounds like basketball sneakers on the court," Liam announces without being asked. I'm just happy that I wasn't hearing things that weren't actually there. Though depending on what the squeaking is, I may prefer a hallucination.

We pause and listen. The squeaking multiplies as it continues to get louder. The air, once tinged with chemicals, now smells musty—like a wet dog after a bath. From out of the darkness comes the first sign of the squeaking source.

"That's no basketball player," Madelyn says as she retreats backward. "It's rats!"

They emerge by the dozens. Like a herd of sheep being guided to one singular location, the rats march toward us. They move in unison, like zombie extras in a horror movie. I don't need to be a rat expert to know that this is not normal rat behavior. Their squeaking intensifies as their whiskers twitch. Their smell is a mixture of ammonia and corn chips. Hundreds of tiny feet shuffle across the concrete floor, and the scraping drowns out the white noise of the pipes.

"They're not coming at us, are they?" I ask, happy to have been born with an irrational fear of snakes as opposed to one of rats. Though, the current circumstances are still not ideal by any means.

Liam points to the horde of oncoming rodents. "Their eyes," he says. "They're not acting of their own free will."

I study the rats as they come closer into view. Liam is right. The rodents' eyes are all pale white and clouded over. We've been doing this long enough to know that this is the unmistakable sign of demonic possession.

"They're under the demon's control," I manage to say as I grab hold of my friends and start to pull them along the tunnel back in the direction that we came. "We need to get out of here."

However, we only make it a few steps before our retreat is quickly halted. Caught in the spotlight of the nearest exit sign, we hear more shuffling against concrete, this time blocking our escape route. It sounds slightly different than the noise caused by the army of rats, though. It's smooth and fluid. Plus, there isn't the scraping of overgrown nails.

"More rats?" Madelyn asks, growing increasingly concerned about what lies just ahead of us in the darkness and the predicament we have found ourselves in.

My eyes widen as they lock in on the first sign of the definitely-not-a-rat. A flicking forked tongue appears in the dim glow, followed by the 20-foot-long serpentine body of a Burmese python.

I feel my stomach sink to the floor.

Did I mention my irrational fear of snakes?

7

"Get behind me," Liam says as he steps between us and the snake. "I got you covered."

After we happened upon a garter snake slithering through the grass one time, Liam learned firsthand about my dislike of the creatures. I had screamed so loud that day that the neighbors ran out of their house thinking that one of us had been seriously injured. Right now, however, I can't seem to find my voice at all. It's the biggest snake I've ever seen.

Liam shakes my shoulder, forcing me to snap out of my trance. "I'll handle the serpent. You two take care of the rats."

Madelyn backs her body against the wall of the tunnel. Her eyes are fixed on the horde of rats. "And how are we supposed to do that exactly?"

The snake reaches Liam's legs, wrapping

itself quickly around his ankles and slithering upward. It constricts as it rises, squeezing and pinning Liam's limbs against himself, first his legs and then his arms. He manages to grab hold of the python's head, even with his arms held tightly against his own body.

"This is a low-level demon we're dealing with," Liam says, though the words are muffled on account of the restricting. The snake is already choking the breath out of my friend. "His possession abilities can't be all that impressive. If they were, he'd have just slipped into the kids' minds and made them do what he wanted. He never would have had to snatch them. You should be able to shake the rats out of the demon's spell."

Madelyn and I stare at Liam as he hand-wrestles the snake's head. The snake opens its jaw wide enough to wrap around Liam's impressive fists. Our expressions must tell Liam that we still don't fully understand his directions because he follows up his initial instructions with a more detailed description. He doesn't seem at all bothered by his direct view into the snake's throat.

"Whack them!" he huffs, the words coming out on an exhale. The snake squeezes even tighter, which keeps Liam from refilling his lungs with more air.

I hear an aggressive squeak coming from within inches of my feet. I glance down to see a rat about to chomp down on my big toe, its yellow teeth raised and at the ready. I react by kicking the critter before it can bite me. The force sends it backward, bowling into the rest of its rodent friends. It slows the horde, and when the kicked rat reemerges from the pile, its eyes are no longer white. They now look like their regular little black marbles.

The rat shakes its head back and forth, clearing the cobwebs from its confused mind. It sprints away into the darkness. This is no longer its fight.

"Liam is right," I say to Madelyn. "Just giving them a whap knocks them out of their trance."

With her back still pressed against the tunnel wall, Madelyn takes a deep breath. She closes her eyes and steadies her nerves. I watch as she presses her hands together and then extends them slowly out in front of herself. She's a certified black belt and has been taking classes at the local dojo since she arrived in Salem.

"I've been training my entire life for this," she says as her eyes snap open. A look of determination washes over her.

Before I can say or do anything, Madelyn springs into action. She moves toward the horde of rats, striking them with her hands and feet. Her movements are fluid, like water running down a rooftop in a rainstorm. It's like I'm watching one of the old kung fu action movies that my dad loves to watch on his rare days off. It's impressive, and I find myself caught up in watching her defeat the rodents.

Each rat Madelyn strikes is pulled out of its possession and sent scurrying in retreat.

I manage to wallop a few rats of my own, though my offense is not nearly as inspiring as Madelyn's. The only thing breathtaking about my toe-poking onslaught is my own breath because the spontaneous fight sequence has left me winded.

I turn to see how Liam is faring with the snake. Although the possessed python continues to constrict him with its muscular body, it's unable to subdue him. Liam is just too strong for it. The viselike grip it has on Liam is faltering.

While the karate lesson continues at my back—was that a flying side kick Madelyn just whipped out?—Liam grabs hold of the snake by the throat with both hands. He rears back and headbutts the python smack-dab between its clouded, white eyes. The snake's body relaxes as it gives up and looks at Liam in complete confusion. The white cloud washes from its eyes, returning them to their normal green globes with black slits.

Blech. I think I preferred them white.

"Welcome back," Liam says to the snake, leaning in to stare deeply into its terrifying eye slits. "Now, what do you say you untangle me before I turn you into a pair of snakeskin boots?"

Snakes can't speak English, but this one seems to fully understand that it is in danger. It unravels itself, releasing its grip on Liam, and falls to the tunnel floor. Without glancing back at us, it slithers away. I breathe a sweet sigh of relief and feel my tense muscles loosen. With the snake gone, I feel myself returning to normal.

Liam and I glance at each other, nod in unison, and immediately turn our attention to the rats. We move forward to defend Madelyn's flanks. She's been doing an admirable job, but the swarming rodents continue to multiply in number and quickly engulf us. We are losing ground. There are just too many of them.

As a group, we start to back away, but the circle of rats only tightens around us. We continue to defend ourselves. We slap, we swipe, we kick, and we claw. It's useless, though. For every rat we send in retreat, two more join the horde.

I had no idea Marblehead had such a serious rat problem.

Just when I think I'll need to be treated

for rabies and whatever other illnesses a wild rat has the potential to carry, I see a shadow skulking above us. Something small and compact emerges from an overhead ventilation shaft and drops down to the tunnel floor. All the rats go instantly still, and their feral faces become frozen in fear. As our luck has it, it's their natural-born enemy that dropped down into the tunnel.

A cat!

8

"Looks like you've got a rat problem, Daddy-O," the cat speaks out of the left side of its mouth.

"You picked a good time to show up," I respond to the cat—which you should know by now is not an ordinary cat.

"You know we've always got your back, Daddy-O."

That voice belongs to Ricky, but there are actually *two* voices inside the cat. The other one belongs to Denise. Ricky and Denise each exist in a different section of the cat's perfectly divided body. The left side has black fur, and that's where Ricky resides. The right side has white fur, and that's where Denise resides. Thankfully, Ricky talks like an extra from a badly scripted 1950s movie, so, while annoying, it at least makes it easy to differentiate between the two.

Ricky and Denise hold up a paw and extend the claws. I see their pearly prickliness glisten in the glow of the nearby exit sign. "We're cool with the rodents, so don't have a hissy fit. We'll TCB this for you. That means take care of business!"

Like a seasoned hunter, the cat turns its sights on the horde of rats and leaps into it with reckless abandon. Guttural growls emerge from the center of the commotion as Ricky and Denise swat at the rats with their paws. The strikes are relentless, like a robot set on automatic destruction.

I know it can be a little confusing. Let me explain more. Ricky and Denise were once teenage boyfriend and girlfriend. This was way back in 1956. They grew up in Salem and started dating during their junior year of high school. Ricky was a hothead—and still is, if I'm being honest—and he liked to spend all of his spare time behind the wheel of his Chevy. He was particularly fond of drag racing. One night, he was challenged to a race. Ricky accepted, even though Denise was strapped into the passenger seat.

With the pedal pressed to the metal, Ricky was already celebrating his victory as he neared the finish line. He couldn't have possibly anticipated that a cat would cross the street at that exact moment. But it did. Without any time to brake, Ricky reacted the only way his fight-or-flight brain could—he jerked the steering wheel to the side. He wrapped his prized Chevy around a tree.

Witnesses said that you couldn't even tell that the pile of twisted metal was even a car anymore. Ricky and Denise both died instantly. Drag racing was banned in Salem. The town mourned their untimely passing, but as it turned out, they never truly left. Their souls have been bound together to that cat ever since. For the last two years, I've been feeding them cans of tuna fish and the occasional dinner table scraps on our back porch. My dad thinks I'm being kind to a stray, but the truth is, I use Ricky and Denise as a source of information. They can go where we can't, which means they can hear what we cannot.

Why they're here in the tunnels beneath Captain Froggerton's Water World, I have no idea, but I'm glad they are.

They are completely shredding the ranks of the rat army, waking them from their possession paralysis with each whack of their paws. The rats are sent fleeing in all directions, their hairless tails tucked between their legs. Before we know it, the vermin have vanished.

The cat sits in the center of the tunnel and begins grooming itself. The entire action comes off as smug and condescending.

"Nothing to be scared of," Ricky says. "You're safe with us, Daddy-O. Heroes for hire, if you dig?"

Yup, definitely smug and condescending.

"What are you two doing down here?" I ask, letting my fingers relax as I release my clenched fists. I shake out my arms, trying to rid myself of the physical stress that my body has been carrying since the arrival of the snake. Seriously, they give me a bad case of the heebie-jeebies.

“We always come down here to hunt,” Denise says from the right side of the cat’s mouth. Her cadence is so much more soothing, and her words are carefully chosen. “Unfortunately, we can’t live on the occasional can of tuna and a random plate of scrambled eggs.”

Gross. I don’t even want to think about what Ricky and Denise have been eating down here. So far, the only options I’ve seen are the rats and a snake that could just as easily eat them.

“The real question is,” Ricky chimes in, “what are you three party poopers doing down here in our stomping grounds?”

Liam steps forward, already annoyed by Ricky’s hotheaded attitude. The funny thing is, Liam and Ricky aren’t that different personality-wise, but you won’t hear me saying that out loud. It’s a revelation I prefer keeping to myself.

“There’s a demon down here snatching up kids,” Liam says, his lips curling upward like a snarling dog. “Maybe you two should consider helping instead of hunting."

Madelyn puts her hand on Liam's shoulder. The action instantly calms him. Her touch is like a cup of tea for Liam's soul.

"Easy, Liam," she says, her voice calm and steady. "Ricky and Denise are friends. We're all on the same side, remember?"

The cat stops grooming and leaps up onto one of the pipes that line the tunnels. Ricky and Denise are now looking at us from our own eye level.

"Children, you say?" Denise questions. "We heard whimpering not far from where we regularly access these tunnels. We didn't think much of it at first—you see all sorts of strange things down here—but now that you mention it, I think it could have been a child's cry."

I step forward. "Can you show us where?"

"As long as the next time we come by your pad, you pop the lid on that top-shelf tuna." The cat takes off down the tunnel, using the pipe as a balance beam.

9

We take all sorts of twists and turns, going deeper into the maze of tunnels. Right, left, left, right, and then I lose track because my ears pick up on the muted cries of a young boy.

"It's just up around this corner," Denise says, leaping down from the pipe.

The tunnel curves in a semicircle and abruptly comes to an end. A closed steel door with a latch for a handle stares back at us. The word *Maintenance* has been stenciled onto the surface of the door, not quite written straight.

I hear the boy's cries coming from the other side of the door.

"Damon, you open it up," Liam says, forming his hands into fists. "I'll rush in first and keep the demon busy while the rest of you get the kids out of there and to safety."

I nod and take hold of the latch. I have to

pull down on it to open the door, which swings out into the tunnels. The hinges are rusted, and the door is a few centimeters too big for the space. I have to muscle it open as it scrapes across the concrete floor. When the gap is big enough, Liam sprints in with his fists at the ready.

Madelyn and I rush in after Liam. The room is large, about the size of a classroom. Our sudden appearance—emphasized by Liam's berserk entrance—causes the two kids inside to scream.

I recognize the boy immediately as the one from the wave pool, even though he is no longer wearing the pirate eye patch. The other is a young girl about the same age. Her blonde hair is pulled back in a tight ponytail, and she is wearing a pair of unicorn flip-flops.

They have a fishing net thrown over them, keeping them in place. Gold coins are spread out on the ground around them, but upon closer inspection, I discover that they're just chocolates wrapped in gold foil paper.

Gary, their demon kidnapper, is not in

the room.

"It's okay," I say in a soothing voice, trying to convince the kids that they don't need to be afraid of us. "We're here to help."

The boy looks up at me, recognition washing over him. "I saw you before. You were in the wave pool, too."

"That's right," I say, pulling the fishing net off the kids. "My name is Damon, and these are my friends, Madelyn and Liam. We're going to get you out of here and back to your parents. You just have to listen to us, okay?"

The kids' fearful expressions turn hopeful.

"What are your names?" Madelyn asks.

"Tommy," the boy says.

The girl responds so quietly that it comes out as a whisper. "Addie."

"It's nice to meet you, Tommy and Addie," I say. "Where is the man who took you?"

Addie's entire body shudders as the color flushes from her face. She is now as white as the possessed rat eyes from earlier.

"He's not a man," she states, each word dripping with fresh fear. "He's a monster. A *real* monster."

I nod, leading both of the kids toward the door. "We know. He happens to be something that my friends and I specialize in. You're safe with us."

Before we can exit into the tunnels, Ricky and Denise pounce into the room, causing the kids to startle. Tommy and Addie both calm down as soon as they realize that the newcomer is a cat . . . at least, until the cat speaks.

"You all need to hurry. Someone is coming this way," Denise says.

The left side of the cat's mouth follows next. "And they're itchin' for a switchin', which means it's time for us to hit the road!"

Tommy and Addie take cover behind me. Liam leans outside of the room and grabs hold of the door. He pulls it shut and then uses his strength to keep anyone from opening it back up. It's not easy barricading a door that opens outward.

"That . . . that cat spoke," Addie says, her voice cracking. After all that these kids have seen and experienced today, a talking cat is probably one step too far for their young brains to wrap around.

I kneel down and look Tommy and Addie in their eyes. I'm suddenly reminded of the time that Dad told me Mom wasn't coming home. I guess even old trauma can feel fresh at times.

"I don't want either of you to worry about the cat," I say, trying to sound reassuring. "They're our friends."

"They?" Tommy asks, equal parts curious and scared.

"It's a long story, but . . ."

BANG

I turn back to look at the door. It bows outward from the frame.

BANG BANG

I watch as Liam's eyes drift down to the latch. It slowly begins to turn downward, manipulated from the other side. Liam wraps both hands around the latch, keeping it from turning any more than it already has.

"Whatever we're doing, we better figure it out fast," he says. "We're about to have some company up in here, and I don't think the space is big enough for the fight we'll need to have to make it out."

10

For the first time since stepping into the room, I spin around and take in every square inch of it. If there's a way to escape, I've got to find it. These kids are depending on me.

"We can't be trapped," I say out loud, though I realize I say it to convince myself. "There has to be a way out."

Just like the tunnels that brought us here, the walls are all slabs of concrete. To the right are a cluster of gauges and meters, each showing a reading of various volts and pressures. To my left is some kind of heating and cooling system. It's a monstrosity of a machine with ductwork stretching from the top of it and branching off in multiple directions.

At the back of the room is an old desk covered in purchase orders and other paperwork. There is a collection of tin figurines—all pirates in various swashbuckling poses—lined up along the backside of the desk. Their paint is chipped and faded, and they look older than the park itself.

A pirate-themed calendar hangs on the wall behind the desk. It isn't turned to the right month. In fact, upon closer inspection, I realize that it's three years old. I guess whoever keeps it hung up just likes the pictures.

Next to the desk is a metal filing cabinet, dented and leaning to one side. On the other side of the cabinet is what appears to be the discarded remains of a maintenance elevator that was never completed. The ceiling is cemented over, just like the rest of the room, and the shaft appears to be boarded up.

"I'm open to any ideas that anyone has," I say, hoping that someone is seeing something that I'm not. "Did you kids notice anything that could help us get out of here? Anything that he might have done while you were watching?"

Addie shakes her head.

“He just kept whistling a song and playing with the figurines on the desk,” Tommy says.

“What song?” Madelyn asks.

Tommy kind of shrugs. “There weren’t any words. But it sounded like something a pirate might sing.”

Ricky and Denise prance over to the unfinished elevator and use their shared nose to sniff at the floor. They’re no bloodhound, but they can certainly pick up on things that we can’t.

“Point those peepers over here, Daddy-O,” Ricky says. “This section of the floor is as thin as those swim trunks of yours.”

As I awkwardly fidget with my shorts, Madelyn runs over to where Ricky and Denise are. She kneels down and knocks on the area of the floor inside the confines of the unfinished elevator.

A cloud of dust forms above the floor. The knock echoes, ringing as if Madelyn were rapping her fist against nothing more than a slim piece of plywood.

“They’re right,” she says optimistically.

"The floor is hollow over here."

BANG BANG

Gary is growing impatient as he tries over and over again to enter the room.

BANG BANG BANG

We're running out of time.

"Everyone search the area to see if it opens up anywhere," I say as I lead Tommy and Addie to the elevator. "Maybe there is a hatch that heads down."

While Liam continues to muscle the door closed, the rest of us search the inside of the elevator's frame for any unseen way of escaping the room.

We tap and pound the hollow floor, testing it for a way out. Ricky and Denise run from corner to corner, checking where the floor meets the walls. None of us turn up anything useful.

I'm sweating, but it's not from the temperature in the room. It's from my nerves.

"Now what?" Madelyn asks, her shoulders sinking.

"I don't suppose anyone has a chainsaw or

a pickax, do they?" I ask half-heartedly.

BANG BANG

"Maybe we could all jump up and down on it?" Tommy asks.

It's actually not a bad idea. If the floor is hollow, which we're pretty sure it is, maybe we can break our way through it. But we'd be taking a big risk. We have no idea what is below this room.

BANG BANG

Then again, it beats being trapped in the room with an angry demon. He's already kidnapped two children and possessed a horde of rats and a giant snake. Who knows what else might he be capable of?

"Everyone jump on three," I say. "One. Two. Three!"

We all leap into the air as I finish the countdown. Our feet return to the floor at the same exact time.

A loud cracking sound fills the room. At first, I think it's Gary, the demon kidnapper, ripping the door off its hinges, so I look in that direction. Liam doesn't say a word. Instead, he shakes his head from side to side and uses his chin to gesture to the floor beneath our feet.

And that's when the floor gives way, and we go from standing . . . to falling.

"Good plan!" I shout to Tommy as we plummet.

11

Tommy and Addie scream as we free fall. I glance down to see a putrid green froth appearing below us just as we splash into an algae-filled body of water.

I sink below the surface, holding my breath just in time. When I finally hit bottom—at least eight feet down—I use my legs to spring myself back up to the surface. My face emerges, and I gasp for air.

"Madelyn?" I call out, panicked to find her hurt or worse.

"Here," her voice declares from behind me.

Now treading water, I spin around to face the other direction and find Madelyn floating in the green pool with a petrified Ricky and Denise clinging to the top of her head. They don't like getting wet any more than a normal cat does.

I am relieved to see Addie floating in the water next to Madelyn.

"Where's Tommy?" I ask, desperation pulling the words from my overtaxed lungs.

Addie points off to her left. I follow the invisible line of her finger to a section of water that is rippling with tiny bubbles. Tommy is down there, but he isn't surfacing. He's drowning.

I inhale, holding the breath in my lungs, and dive. I kick to motor myself downward, though even with my eyes open, I can't see a thing. The water is too murky.

I feel along the bottom with my hands. It's gravelly and rough to the touch. I tap along the underwater floor with my fingers, searching and searching until I eventually discover a foot. I follow the foot to its knee, then its abdomen, and finally a shoulder.

I slip my hands beneath the arms and swim up as fast as I can. Up, up, up, and . . .

GASP

Tommy and I break the surface of the murky water, bobbing up and down like chunks of meat in a hearty stew. Madelyn and Addie swim to us as we try to recapture our breaths.

"Are you okay?" I ask Tommy.

Exhausted, tears fill his eyes. All he can do is nod his head. He may be okay physically, but this entire ordeal has taken its toll on him emotionally—and rightfully so.

I spin and look around as I tread water. Wherever we are is a lot older than the Captain Froggerton's tunnels.

This place, which is more of a cavern than a room, looks like some kind of decommissioned subway tunnel. One thing is for certain, though—the water doesn't belong here. No, this green sludge was purposefully placed here, a subway tunnel turned into some kind of demonic wave pool. But why?

"Are you guys okay down there?" I hear Liam call out from above us.

I glance up at the hole in the ceiling—the same one we fell through. It's about ten or so feet to the room where Liam is still trapped, now by himself.

“We’re okay,” I shout back, spitting more of the gross water out of my mouth. “We landed in some kind of swimming pool.”

“Our friend has stopped trying to push the door open,” he says. “I’m starting to think that we might have fallen right into his trap. Or at least, you all did.”

I spin around frantically, searching for any sign of the demon. “Maybe you should get down here with us then. We’re sitting ducks in this water, and there’s nowhere for us to climb out and stand.”

I hear footsteps from above us—sprinting footsteps.

“Belly flop!” Liam bellows as he leaps down through the hole in the ceiling.

We watch in a combination of awe and horror as Liam drops out of the sky horizontally and slaps down onto the surface of the green water.

A massive splash originates at the point of impact and soaks all of us, including Ricky and Denise, who have until now somehow managed to stay dry. They hiss at the rippling section of water where Liam entered.

"That friend of yours is a real nosebleed," Ricky says with a scowl, or as close to a scowl as a cat can make.

An exuberant Liam bursts out of the water with a big grin on his face. He lifts up his shirt to reveal a bright red chest and stomach. His belly flop has left him with what looks like a serious sunburn. Once a trickster, always a trickster.

"Good thing this is just a meat suit I'm wearing because that dive is definitely going to leave a mark," he says, chuckling to himself.

Tommy coughs, clearing his throat. "What do you mean that you're wearing a 'meat suit'?"

I want to curse Liam out for finding fun in this nightmare of a water park trip, but I stop myself. Tommy and Addie need some confident coolness that they can latch onto until we can get them safely out of here.

They don't need to see me going off on Liam. All that will do is make them panic. As will describing what is beneath Liam's layer of human skin. Not that he's ever shown me what is under there. But I've seen enough demons to appreciate that it likely isn't as good-looking as the "meat suit."

"He's just kidding," I say. "Ignore him."

Liam's smile slowly fades. Our silence is enough to tell him that his antics are not appreciated at the current moment in time, even if I am silently impressed with the near-perfect form of his belly flop.

My eyes drift down from Liam's face to where his body disappears into the gloomy water. Floating freely beside him, rocking up and down on the ripples cresting across the surface of the pool, is a half-eaten cucumber.

And that's when it dawns on me. The drifting cucumber makes me realize why this old tunnel is filled with water and why Tommy and Addie were taken from their parents and brought down here. It is so obvious, yet we somehow missed it. All of us.

"I know what we're dealing with," I say, still treading water but feeling my body growing increasingly tired. "There's only one type of demon I know of who enjoys snacking on cucumbers. The evidence was right there from the moment I spotted his aura. The maintenance man who took the kids, he's a kappa!"

12

"What's a kappa?" Addie asks, now holding onto Madelyn's back for extra buoyancy.

Madelyn reaches out and grabs the cucumber. "They're a type of kami. That's a kind of water spirit."

Addie lets out a breath so powerful that it seems to be forced from her body. She's frightened again. "Like . . . like . . . a ghost?"

"That's us, kitty cat," Ricky says, shaking the water from their fur. "We two go boo. No, the thing that has its peepers set on you is a demon."

Neither Addie nor Tommy know how to respond to that. I shoot Ricky a glare, letting him know that I don't appreciate him scaring the kids any more than they already are. He looks away, either embarrassed by what he's done or uninterested in my criticism.

Beneath the surface, I feel a shift in the water as it seems to be pulled in one direction. There's now a current where there wasn't one before. And that's not all.

"Do you hear that?" Denise asks. Her cat ears pivot like satellites in the direction of the perceived sound. "It's like . . . sink water running down the drain."

Yes, that's exactly what it is. That's why the water is suddenly pulling to the right. Someone is draining the subway tunnel.

We all huddle together, our backs facing inward so that we can cover all sides.

"Everyone stay alert," I say. "Kappas are at home in the water. It could be anywhere."

We wait for the demon to appear, but there's still no sign of it. Minutes pass as the water level slowly sinks.

"What do we know about kappas?" I ask as the bottom becomes visible through the green filter of the water. "Other than them snacking on cucumbers for fun."

Madelyn is the first to respond. "We've never faced one, so I have never done much research on them. What I know from my minimal reading on the breed is that they're aquatic, reptilian in appearance, and known for causing playful mischief."

"I think we're beyond playful mischief," Liam huffs as the water has drained enough from the tunnel for him to find his footing.

Madelyn looks at him and scowls. "By all means then, Liam, share some of your wisdom with the rest of us."

Liam shakes his head. "Can't. I've never come across one myself, not in The Pit or up here topside. However, I'll contribute plenty by punching it in its face when it finally does decide to show itself."

Tommy tugs on my arm. "What's The Pit?" he asks.

"Just the nickname for the town that Liam is from," I respond. There's no need to get into a lesson about where demons are from.

It takes at least ten minutes, but the last of the water finally spills down into a large open grate on the side of the tunnel. That's where I spot Gary crouched down. He has a toy pirate sword stuck upside down in the drain.

Was he in the water with us the entire time?

"I don't think you're going to have to wait much longer for that particular contribution," I say, pulling Tommy and Addie behind me so that they're not in the direct path of the demon. "He's decided to join the party."

Gary slowly rises. He says nothing.

"Don't let him get us," Addie pleads. I can feel her entire body trembling out of fear.

"That ain't happening!" Liam says, stepping toward Gary.

Liam's forward progress is quickly brought to a pause as Gary raises his hand. Liam is extra cautious, unsure how he should proceed without understanding what kind of powers a kappa has. All we know is that it can possess rats and has a hankering for the occasional cucumber. It's not a ton of information to go on.

"Anyone know what I should expect from him after I hit him for the first time?" Liam asks.

Madelyn and I shake our heads. Gary could turn into Captain Froggerton's Zigzagging Lazy River and take us upstream for all we know.

Instead, we watch, ready to react, as Gary extends a thumb and then pops it into his mouth like a lollipop. With his other hand, he reaches up and pinches his nose closed and then . . . blows.

Liam raises an eyebrow. "What is happening here exactly?"

I don't answer because I can't. Instead, I watch, dumbfounded, as Gary continues to forcefully blow against his thumb. As he does, his human flesh expands around him, inflating like a balloon. He continues to blow and swell until . . .

POP

Gary's human costume bursts, shattering into a plume of human particles. The parts and pieces that were once a wrinkled maintenance man rain down around us. One of Gary's ears lands on my shoulder. I quickly swat it away, my mind still associating anything slimy with the snake.

"I don't know what I expected, but it was way more than this," Liam says as he eyeballs what remains of Gary, now in his demon form.

Standing beside the open grate is a three-foot-tall humanoid creature with scaly green skin, webbed hands and feet, and a shell that protrudes from his back. The shell is more like an ornate hermit crab shell than a turtle shell. The creature's head is no bigger than a coconut, which comes to a sharpened point at his beak. His eyes are small and round, looking like a pair of hard candies that seem pushed into position within his scaly flesh.

But the strangest thing about Gary is that he has a slight indentation on top of his head. It looks like a bowl, and it's filled with water.

If I didn't already know he was a kidnapping demon, I'd go so far as to describe Gary as adorable.

Liam laughs at the sight of the creature. "The only thing impressive about you is your smell," he says, rubbing his nose to try and rid it of the foul scent.

It's true. If I were bottling up Gary's aroma as a perfume, I'd call it Octopus Farts.

The creature's beak opens. "Gary," it says. The name comes out like a gargle, as if his throat is filled with water. There's nothing outwardly threatening about what is said or how it's said, but that doesn't stop the kids from being creeped out. They back away, huddling closer together.

Liam raises his hand in front of himself, positioning his body in a classic boxer's stance. "Yeah, I don't need your name to knock you out, man," he says dismissively. "So do me a favor and just keep standing there while I give you one of my patented knuckle dusters!"

Instead of standing still like a punching bag, though, Gary surges forward with race-car-like speed, driving his forehead into Liam's chest. Liam is knocked off his feet and sent flying backward through the air. He crashes through the wall of the subway tunnel, where he is engulfed in a cloud of dust and debris.

I'd be concerned if I didn't know that Liam's demon strength makes him as durable as a rubber mallet.

"Well, pop my bubble gum; this baddie daddy can get off the line quicker than my Chevy could," Ricky declares.

It's a good reminder that we should never underestimate our opponents, not even ones as adorable as Gary.

13

I feel one of the kids tugging on the back of my shirt. I keep my eyes on the kappa but address the attention-grabbing tug.

"Yup?" I say simply.

It's Tommy's voice that responds. "I play an RPG where one of the boss monsters looks *exactly* like that. It even has that weird little bowl of water built into its head."

For those out of the tabletop gaming loop, RPG stands for role-playing game. Usually, these immersive games are filled with wizards and elves and dragons. This is my first time hearing about one that features a kappa.

I turn to Tommy, taking my eyes off the demon. I trust that Madelyn will keep hers fixed on him for the both of us. "How do you beat the monster in the game?"

Before Tommy can answer the question,

Gary has surged to where we are standing, grabbing the kids and then quickly pulling them away. He has both Tommy and Addie tucked underneath his arms. Because they're taller than Gary, the kids have to stand in a squat. Gary's strength keeps them this way.

"Gary," he says as he fixes his gumball eyes on me.

A wave of terror washes over me. I'm so scared to fail these kids that I lose sight of my own safety. I reach out, grab Addie by the hand, and try to reel her in, but the kappa is just too strong. He pulls both of the kids alongside him toward the drain and pulls the plastic sword from it. He brandishes it out in front of himself, pointing the tip toward me as if it were an *actual* weapon.

The demon's eyes take on a new shape—somewhat triangular with sharp edges. They change color, too, going from a nondescript neutral to the kind of red that exists to make a point. It's unnerving.

"Gary!" he says again, and somehow, I know this is the last warning the kappa is going to give me.

I feel my eyes tear up. "I am not letting you take those kids."

The kappa's head slowly twists to the side as he spins Tommy and Addie away. He is now giving me his full attention. The hairs on the back of my neck stand up, my entire being chilled to the core by the creature's gaze. I have never felt more in the crosshairs of something so dangerous before. Which, in my line of work, is saying a lot.

"Gary," he says nonchalantly and shrugs his shoulders. I guess he is at peace with whatever he has decided to do to me.

Thankfully, I don't have to find out what that is.

"Belly flop!" I hear Liam shout from slightly above where we are standing.

I look up to see Liam leaping out of the hole in the subway tunnel wall. It happens so quickly—and is such an unorthodox style of attack—that Gary is unable to get out of the way in time. Liam lands belly-down on top of the kappa, using the first-ever battle belly flop in the history of the world, at least as far as I know.

As Liam wrestles with the demon, I run to collect Tommy and Addie. I repeat my question to Tommy, hoping to get an answer this time.

"Quick, how do you beat the monster in the game?"

Tommy looks out at the kappa as Liam tries unsuccessfully to pin the demon to the ground before looking back at me. "You have to challenge him to a fight. He will always accept because he refuses to be embarrassed by a human."

Madelyn joins us. Ricky and Denise are now standing on her shoulders, still not happy with the amount of water lingering around at our feet.

"Our friend is wrestling with him now," Madelyn says. "How is the fight in the game any different from what Liam is doing?"

Tommy clears his throat. "It doesn't matter how strong you are. It doesn't matter what kind of spells or potions you're carrying.

You'll never defeat him like that. You have to outsmart him."

"I don't understand, Tommy," I say. "Outsmart him how?"

He points over at the kappa. Gary is slapping Liam with the flat side of the plastic sword. "See that water in the dent on his head? You have to make him spill it out. All of it. That's the source of his power."

A look of determination washes over Madelyn. I've known her long enough to know that she was born with a Texas-sized bravery organ. Whether that's the brain or the heart, I'm not sure, but I know that Madelyn has a surplus of both. So much so that I've had to talk her out of numerous acts of courageous bravado in the past.

"Whatever you're thinking of doing," I say, "I want you to push it out of your mind right now."

Madelyn looks away from the scuffle taking place between the two demons and scowls at me. Her spine goes rigid. The shift in her posture causes Ricky and Denise to lose their balance and they fall down to the ground. The cat splashes into a puddle, much to the dismay of the two souls inside.

"I don't need your permission to play my part on this team," she tells me. "I am perfectly capable of whatever I set my mind to achieving."

I reach out and grab Madelyn's hands. I squeeze them. It's a hug for the hands. "Of course you are. I would never question that. But that kappa is stronger than it looks. Even Liam is having a difficult time dealing with its strength, even if it's just slapping him with that toy sword. I just . . ." I pause, looking away from her before finishing my thought. "I don't want you to get hurt."

Madelyn squeezes my hands back, acknowledging my concern for her well-being. I release her hands, and she raises them, swiping the wet hair away from her face. She tucks the white-blond strands behind each of her ears.

"I'm not going to fight the demon," she says. "You heard Tommy. I just have to outsmart it. And thanks to my karate training, I have the agility and strength to do it."

Madelyn turns away from me and looks out at Liam and Gary as they continue to grapple. Liam currently has the kappa's tiny head in a headlock and is doing his best to wrench it upside down. No matter what Liam does, however, the bowl on Gary's head remains upright.

"Liam!" Madelyn shouts assertively. "Let him go!"

Liam looks up, the kappa's head still locked under his arm. "Huh? No way! It will attack you and snatch the kids."

Madelyn shakes her head. "No, it won't. Because I challenge it to a physical contest."

14

"Gary?" the kappa says, looking up at us as he remains framed in the nook of Liam's arm.

"Ain't happening!" Liam says. "I heard what Tommy said, and I can get the job done just fine on my own. I'm not letting this little bugger go until I spill every last drop of his head juice."

Madelyn steps forward. She rests a hand on Liam's shoulder. Once again, her voice is like a lullaby that soothes the darkest side of Liam's demon nature.

"It's okay, Liam. Let him go."

Hesitantly, Liam cautiously recoils his arm from around Gary's head. His hands remain clenched into fists, expecting to have to defend himself or us from a surprise kappa onslaught, but it never comes.

Gary straightens himself upright and waves

his plastic sword in the air. He never takes his gumball eyes off of Madelyn. "Gary."

I'm not sure if Madelyn can understand Gary, but she makes it seem like she does. "That's right. I challenge you to best me."

The kappa's beak opens and closes, excitedly snapping. Gary drops the toy sword and lowers his head, making sure to keep the bowl upright. He points his forehead directly at Madelyn and I anticipate a battering ram charge will come at any moment.

Madelyn holds up her hand, halting the kappa's attack. "Not so fast. I don't challenge you to a fight. I challenge you to a handstand competition. Whoever stays up in the air the longest wins."

I can't hide my smile. For as brave as Madelyn is, she's twice as smart. Her plan to defeat the kappa is ingenious. I've seen her do a handstand plenty of times before, and I'm confident that she can defy gravity long enough to drain Gary's bowl of every last drop.

The kappa marches from side to side. He's agitated but also conflicted. I know because he no longer seems interested in Tommy and Addie. He is fully focused on Madelyn and the challenge that she has issued.

"Gary," Gary says, slapping himself on the head. I can't be sure, but I think he's trying to psyche himself up, like a gym bro working up to max out on bench press day. "Gary! Gary! Gary!"

Madelyn highlights the stakes of the competition for the kappa. "If we win, we walk out of here with the kids. And you can't do a thing about it, understand?"

"And if he wins?" Liam asks nervously.

The kappa turns his head to look at Tommy and Addie. He opens his beak and hisses out the now all-too-familiar word—the only one it can say—but this time, it means *something* to all of us. "Gary."

I swallow hard. The stakes are high. If Gary takes the kids, they'll probably never be seen or heard from again.

I believe in Madelyn, but does she believe in herself? Are her arms tired from treading water? Is the floor slippery from the puddles?

What if the liquid in the kappa's bowl is thicker than water, and it oozes instead of pours? Can she outlast him then?

Okay, maybe I am a little nervous about Madelyn being able to pull this off after all.

"I'll go first," Madelyn instructs. "Damon, you track it with your phone. Whatever time I get, Gary just has to beat that if he wants to win."

I fish the sandwich bag containing my phone out of my swim trunks. I type in my security code, and the phone glows. Swiping my thumb across the screen, I locate my stopwatch app and open it. I can't believe the fate of the mission is coming down to a handstand contest.

"All set," I say. My thumb hovers over the button.

Madelyn nods and then looks for a suitable location—one that is mostly dry and even ground. She stretches out her shoulders and shakes out her arms.

Liam steps in front of Gary and points directly in his face. His finger is practically touching the kappa's beak.

"And no interfering," he adds as if the competition's instructions were still being spelled out. "If you break her concentration, I break your beak."

Gary completely ignores Liam and his threat. The kappa remains focused on Madelyn, who, at that exact moment, is pressing her palms down into the subway tunnel's floor.

"Start the timer as soon as I get my feet in the air," she tells me.

I nod. And with that, Madelyn swings her feet into the air with just enough momentum to keep them positioned directly above her head. Her legs then splay outward in opposing directions, separating like a pair of scissors.

I press the start button with my thumb, and the stopwatch springs to life, spitting out numbers on the screen as it tracks Madelyn's handstand stamina.

Three seconds.

Everyone is silent. All I can hear are the heavy breaths from our anxious group, along with the eager snapping of the kappa's beak.

Five seconds.

Madelyn's legs spread outward a bit more as she does her best to maintain her balance.

Eight seconds.

Ricky and Denise begin to groom themselves. Is it just me, or is this completely inappropriate timing? I figure it must be a nervous tic that brings the two souls inside the cat some level of comfort.

Ten seconds.

A milestone, but signs of fatigue are beginning to show themselves. Madelyn has now closed her eyes for extra concentration, and her arms have begun to shake and shudder. Her muscles are feeling the strain.

Thirteen seconds.

Lucky thirteen. I feel good about her time, but my confidence shrinks when I look over at the kappa.

Gary is unimpressed by Madelyn's handstand sustainability. Maybe it's just his demon ego, but what if he knows something that we don't? What if Tommy's game is just that . . . a game? In hindsight, maybe we shouldn't have bet everything on a story from a kid's RPG.

Seventeen seconds.

Madelyn's legs come back together and fall forward. The rest of her body follows, and she topples over. Her knees smack down onto the floor of the subway tunnel, and she lifts her head, a hopeful expression aimed in my direction.

"Seventeen seconds," I tell her, holding up my phone for everyone to see. "That's seventeen *more* seconds than I could hold a handstand for. Nicely done."

The kappa leaps up and down wildly, hopping in place. He points his beak in my direction, still hopping as he speaks. "Gary."

I take that as my cue to restart the stopwatch. I refresh the screen and hover my thumb over the start button.

Gary watches this and then springs into action—*literally* springing up into the air and landing upside down in a perfect handstand.

It's news to me, but apparently, a kappa's

neck is extremely flexible because even upside down, Gary manages to keep his head upright. Not a single drop has spilled out from the bowl.

Three seconds.

15

I look back at Tommy and Addie. Their fearful faces cause my heart to wrench. We can't fail them.

Five seconds.

I scan the room, looking for any kind of assistance. Would it be too much to ask for a sudden natural disaster to strike this abandoned subway tunnel? Something that could shake the kappa's balance? An earthquake, perhaps?

Eight seconds.

The clock is ticking, and nothing is spilling. Not a single driblet of head liquid. And worse yet, Gary is showing no sign of getting tired. By the looks of it, he could hold this handstand all day.

Ten seconds.

The kappa begins to chuckle. His gargling

voice repeats "Gary, Gary, Gary," but it comes out like laughter. Is he mocking us or having fun?

Thirteen seconds.

Gary is going to beat Madelyn's time. There is no doubt about it. We're going to fail. The kids will have to go off to who knows where with the demon, and I'm not sure if we can stop it from happening.

Without any prompting from the rest of us, Ricky and Denise go and sit down directly in front of Gary. They pick back up on grooming themselves, this time only inches from the kappa's face.

Okay, this is *definitely* inappropriate timing.

Gary's body curls slightly inward, and out of nowhere, he releases a violent sneeze that causes his handstand to falter. More importantly, the upside-down sneeze forces all of the water inside of the bowl on his head to expel outward. Ricky and Denise are covered in the liquid as Gary topples over.

I press stop on the stopwatch. "Sixteen seconds," I say in disbelief. "You did it,

Madelyn! You beat him!"

With his belly pressed into the ground, the defeated kappa looks out in horror at the puddle of spilled water. "Gary?"

We celebrate, jumping up and down and congratulating Madelyn on her victory. Although happy that she has won Tommy and Addie their freedom, she is reluctant to sing her own praise. She knows that she didn't win the challenge on her own.

Madelyn turns to Ricky and Denise. "You knew the kappa would sneeze. How?"

The cat leaps up onto Madelyn's shoulders and speaks out of the right side of its mouth. "Actually, we didn't. We hoped that would be the case, though. If there is one thing we've learned since becoming a cat, it's that a lot of people are allergic to us. And apparently, demons, too."

Perched on Madelyn's shoulders, the cat turns to look at me. It's now Ricky's turn to speak. "And I'd say our keen illuminations are worth at least a week of that top-shelf tuna. Don't you agree, Daddy-O?"

"At least," I say in agreement. I reach out and pat the cat's head, which, to my surprise, is well received. There is even some purring.

We're about to turn around and try to find our way out of this maze of tunnels when the kappa screams, capturing all of our attention.

"Gary!" he cries out, his beak falling open.

We all watch as the kappa tries desperately to cup the spilled water into his hands and return it to the bowl on his head. It's a pointless act, given that most of the water is now saturating Ricky and Denise's fur. I know because I just ran my hand through it.

"What is he doing?" Addie asks.

I take one step closer, trying to decipher Gary's frenzied behavior. "I don't know. No one is this much of a sore loser."

Madelyn chimes in. "Tommy said that the water in the bowl was the source of the kappa's power. Maybe that means it is his life force . . . the thing that is actually keeping him alive and here in our realm."

I silently ponder what this means for the fate of the kappa. Sure, he kidnapped the children, which is beyond wrong. And he was violent with us. But still, something about Gary seems different than most of the demons we usually face. Most want to murder first and ask questions later.

The kappa extends his hand behind himself—again with incredible flexibility—and reaches into the space between his own shell and his back. He digs around inside for a few seconds and pulls something out. It's Tommy's pirate eye patch, minus the elastic band that holds it to the head.

"Gary," the kappa says quietly as he reaches out to hand the eye patch to me.

I take the eye patch in my hand and look down at it. A million thoughts speed through my brain before settling on one that makes more sense than I want it to, given how things are playing out.

"He wasn't going to hurt them," I say, the words coming out robotic and without the glee expressed during our recent celebration.

"What are you talking about?" Liam says, pointing to a gash in his side where the kappa's beak cut him. “He hurt me no problem. He was certainly going to hurt the kids.”

I kneel down so that I’m at eye level with Gary. I shake my head. “No. He was just playing a part, just like I was in the wave pool. He was pretending to be a pirate. The old tin figurines on the desk, the toy sword, the chocolate coins . . . he was role-playing, just like an RPG game.”

“Gary,” he says as his vibrant green skin fades and turns brown.

“He was playing with them,” I continue, my voice cracking.

We watch as the kappa goes through a painful transformation, like a leaf going from healthy in the spring to brittle in the fall. His flesh becomes dry as flakes peel away and drift off into the air. He holds up his hand and extends his thumb.

“No,” I say, trying to stop Gary from going any further, even though I know it’s not his choice to make. We already made that choice for him.

Gary sticks his thumb into his mouth

and blows.

I turn to Liam and Madelyn. "Get the kids out of here."

Liam hesitates. "But . . ."

"Just do it!" I bark, having a difficult time keeping my emotions in check.

Liam and Madelyn collect Tommy and Addie and lead them out of the tunnel through the hole in the wall. Ricky and Denise stay with me, which I appreciate.

I sit down next to Gary and reach out to rest my hand on his beak. The least I can do is comfort him as he takes his last kappa breath.

I'm not sure how much time passes because it feels like time is standing still. Ricky and Denise don't say a word. They're just as caught up in our error in judgment as I am. I am ashamed. I am heartbroken.

16

I stay seated at Gary's side as he blows flake after flake of himself out into the universe until there is nothing left of him.

When the final sliver of Gary falls to the ground and dissolves into a puddle of green water, I lower my head and whisper an apology.

"I'm sorry for not trying to understand you," I say. "I'm sorry for not giving you a chance."

Ricky and Denise reach out with a paw and rest it on my knee. "We couldn't have been plugged into his reasoning, Daddy-O," Ricky says, trying to comfort me. "We don't speak kappa."

I pick up the cat and place Ricky and Denise on my shoulders. I stand and make my way toward the hole in the subway tunnel wall where we meet up with Liam, Madelyn, and the kids.

"No, but even if we did, I'm not so sure we would have heard him anyway."

It takes us a while, but eventually, we make our way out of the tunnels and back up the concrete stairs to the supply shed. No one says a word on the entire trip back.

We bring Tommy and Addie over to the security guards. Tommy's mom scoops him up in her arms and squeezes him tightly.

"Tommy!" she wails. "Where were you?"

Addie's dad kneels down and hugs her close. He starts to cry.

"Are you okay?" he asks her. "Are you hurt?"

Addie shakes her head. "I'm fine."

The Lily Pad officers are relieved. They inform the Frog Pond that "disaster has been averted."

The police, on the other hand, have a few questions for us. We tell them that we saw the kids wander off into the tunnels and went after them instead of letting any adults know.

"Why wouldn't you bring it to someone's

attention?" one of them asks suspiciously. She doesn't seem to believe our story.

I shrug my shoulders. "I guess I'm just used to watching my dad solve problems, so I tend to try and solve them myself as well."

It's a fib I've told dozens of times since we started hunting demons. For whatever reason, when you tell people that your dad is a police officer, they tend to give you a pass when it comes to your motives for doing good.

"You look familiar," she says with a raised eyebrow. "What's your name?"

After I tell her, the officer's expression completely changes. Her suspicion turns to warmth.

"Your dad is a good man," she tells me. "I just took a training seminar with him. Sharp as a tack, that one is. I guess the apple didn't fall too far from the tree."

Her expression changes again, going from warmth to sympathy.

"I was real sorry to hear about your mom," she tells me, resting a hand on my shoulder.

After that, the investigation is quickly

buttoned up and we are sent on our way.

We still have two hours before Madelyn's mom is scheduled to pick us up. None of us feel all that interested in continuing our "fun" day at Captain Froggerton's Water World, though.

Instead, Madelyn calls her mom and asks her to pick us up early. We are in her car and on our way back to Salem within twenty minutes.

"Did we do the right thing?" Madelyn whispers as we're all tucked in side by side in the backseat.

I shrug. "The kids are safe. That has to be enough. Otherwise, I'm going to start questioning everything we've done since the day we started demon hunting."

Liam wriggles in his seat, trying to give himself more space. With the three of us crammed in shoulder to shoulder, his adult-sized body is stuck like a sardine in a tin can.

"I'm questioning agreeing to sit in the middle between you two," he says, grunting and groaning. "I can barely breathe in here."

I roll down my window to let some fresh

air flow in. Although it's a hot summer breeze, it's still cooler than what Liam grew up feeling on his face in The Pit. The puffs of air seem to calm him.

Madelyn's mom pulls the car out of the parking lot.

"Did you kids have fun today?" she asks in her distinctive southern drawl. "I saw the police were here. Anything go wrong?"

So much went wrong, but one of the burdens we carry as demon hunters is that we can't talk about it with the adults in our lives. That was one rule we all agreed to when we started hunting. It's hard, but necessary. We want to keep our parents safe.

"Yeah," Madelyn says cheerfully. "Some kids wandered off, but they were found safe and sound. I guess in that regard, it was a good day."

Madelyn's mom looks up into the rearview mirror at us.

"But you didn't have fun?"

"No, we did," Madelyn responds. "It's just that . . ."

“There were really long lines,” I say, finishing Madelyn’s fabricated thought for her. “We just got impatient.”

Madelyn’s mom nods her head. She buys the story that we’re selling.

We all look out at Captain Froggerton’s Water World as we pass by along the road. Rising above the park is the Devil’s Plunge waterslide. It has a massive drop that descends into a dark cavern.

The person riding it flies down at an alarming speed and emerges out of the cavern into a shallow pool. It looks terrifying, and I instantly regret that we didn’t get a chance to take the plunge ourselves.

“We still have to ride the Devil’s Plunge before the end of the summer,” I say. “It’s on our summer to-do list.”

Liam nods. “We’ll come back when it’s not as busy. And when we do, we’ll all dress like pirates.”

“In honor of our new friend?” I ask quietly.

Liam smiles at me and nods. “In honor of our new friend.”

ABOUT THE AUTHOR

When not writing in his spiral notebooks, Jason M. Burns can be found outside getting his tattoo-covered arms dirty where he spends the warmer months hybridizing daylilies and tending to his koi pond. Type A even when typing, he has written and created a number of critically-acclaimed and commercially successful comic book series and graphic novels, including *Magical Pet Vet* and *Jericho: Season 3*, which appeared on the *New York Times* Best Sellers list. He has spearheaded book lines for *Sesame Street* and the DreamWorks Animation stable of titles and most recently served as Chief Creative Officer for Neymar Jr. Comics, the publishing company of international soccer star Neymar Jr. There his writing was translated across six languages and reached over forty million people worldwide. In addition to comic books, Burns also works in Hollywood where he has a number of television and film projects in development. He is also co-host of the popular podcast series *What About*, which he produces alongside actor Danny Nucci (*Titanic*, *The Fosters*).

Burns lives in Massachusetts with his wife, two children, and a trio of rescue dogs with unnecessarily silly names, Bark W. Grizwold, Maisy Gray, and Bad Bad Leroy Brown.